Yankee Doodle

Yan-kee Doo-dle went to town, Rid-ing on a po-ny,

Stuck a feath-er in his cap, and called it mac-a-ro-ni.

Chorus

Yan-kee Doo-dle, keep it up, Yan-kee Doo-dle dan-dy,

Mind the mus-ic and the step, and with the girls be han-dy.

YANKEE DOODLE

YANKEE
STEVEN

DOODLE
KELLOGG

SIMON & SCHUSTER BOOKS FOR YOUNG READERS

SIMON & SCHUSTER BOOKS FOR YOUNG READERS

An imprint of Simon & Schuster Children's Publishing Division

1230 Avenue of the Americas

New York, NY 10020

Illustrations copyright © 1976, 1996 by Steven Kellogg

All rights reserved including the right of reproduction
in whole or in part in any form.

SIMON & SCHUSTER BOOKS FOR YOUNG READERS
is a trademark of Simon & Schuster.

The text of this book is set in 21-point Dutch 823.

Book design by Anahid Hamparian

Manufactured in the United States of America

Second Edition

10 9 8 7 6 5 4 3 2

Library of Congress Cataloging-in-Publication Data

[Yankee Doodle]

Steven Kellogg's Yankee Doodle

      p.   cm.

Summary: An illustrated version of the well-known song of the American Revolution.

ISBN 0-689-80158-0

1. Childen's songs—United States—Texts. 2. United States—History—Revolution, 1775-1783—Songs and music.

[1. Songs—United States. 2. United States—History—Revolution, 1775-1783—Songs and music.]

I. Kellogg, Steven, ill. II. Title. III. Title: Yankee Doodle.

PZ8.3.B223Yan   1996   782.42164'0268—dc20   [E]   94-23603

For Edward Tucker Jr.

Yankee Doodle went to town,
riding on a pony,

Stuck a feather in his hat
and called it macaroni.

Yankee Doodle, keep it up, Yankee Doodle dandy,
Mind the music and the step, and with the girls be handy.

Father and I went down to camp,
along with Captain Good'in,
And there we saw the men and boys
as thick as hasty puddin'.

And there we saw a thousand men
as rich as Squire David;

And what they wasted ev'ry day,
I wish it could be sav'ed.

Yankee Doodle, keep it up, Yankee Doodle dandy,
Mind the music and the step, and with the girls be handy.

And there I saw a little keg,
its head all made of leather,
They knocked on it with little sticks
to call the folks together.

And there was Captain Washington
upon a slapping stallion,
A-giving orders to his men—
I guess there was a million.

And the ribbons on his hat,
they looked so very fine, ah!
I wanted peskily to get
to give to my Jemima.

Yankee Doodle, keep it up, Yankee Doodle dandy,

Mind the music and the step, and with the…

And there I saw a swamping gun,
large as a log of maple.
Upon a mighty little cart—
a load for father's cattle.

And every time they fired it off,
it took a horn of powder,

It made a noise like father's gun,
only a nation louder!

The troopers, too, would gallop up
and fire right in our faces,

It scared me almost half to death
to see them run such races.

I saw another snarl of men,
a-digging graves, they told me,

So 'tarnal long, so 'tarnal deep,
they 'tended they should hold me.

It scared me so I hooked it off,
nor stopped, as I remember,

Nor turned about till I got home,
locked up in Mother's chamber.

Yankee Doodle, keep it up,

Yankee Doodle dandy,

Mind the music and the step,

and with the girls be handy.

A NOTE ABOUT YANKEE DOODLE

Year after year, on the Fourth of July, generations of patriots in the United States parade to the high-spirited stanzas and chorus of *Yankee Doodle* in tribute to this country's struggle for independence during the Revolutionary War. But did you ever wonder exactly where the song came from? Who wrote it? And what it is all about?

Many people are surprised to hear that the tune was actually sung by the British at the beginning of the American Revolution (1775–1783) to poke fun at the colonists. (A "Yankee" is an old-fashioned name for people from New England, and the word "doodle" originally meant *to ridicule.*) Some attribute the song's authorship to Dr. Richard Shackburg, a surgeon in the British army, who may have heard several of the many variations of lyrics to a tune that had been sung in the colonies since the French and Indian War (1754–1763). When England's King George III sent his red-coated troops to make the colonists obey laws that they felt were unfair, it is said that the British bands played *Yankee Doodle*—mockingly, no doubt—as their ships arrived.

But in the nineteenth century, one musicologist declared that the song was definitely Yankee—not British—in its dialect, and he credited the song lyrics that we sing today to a member of the class of 1777 at Harvard College, Edward Bangs, who served as a minuteman at the Battle of Lexington during his sophomore year. Bangs may have rewritten the earlier Yankee song with a new hero, a naive and inquisitive young patriot, then printed it on a broadside as a rousing war song titled "The Yankee's Return from Camp." As the song's popularity grew, the American troops reclaimed it as their own, playing it triumphantly when the British general Cornwallis surrendered at Yorktown in 1781.

Even after the Revolutionary War ended, the jaunty tune just wouldn't go away. Not only was it again used as a battle song during the Mexican War (1846–1848) but it was also played and sung in theaters—and if the audiences didn't get to hear it, sometimes they called for it. The song was also borrowed for

The word "macaroni" did not always refer to just a type of pasta. It also meant a group of young, well-traveled Englishmen who often wore fancy trimmings on their hats and clothing. The trimming itself then became known as macaroni.

"Hasty puddin'" (pudding) is a thick porridge made of boiled water and flour, oatmeal, or cornmeal.

A "keg" is a small barrel— in this story, it is used as a makeshift musical instrument.